Story © 1985 by Essei Okawa
Illustrations © 1985 by Teruyo Endo

First Printing 1985

Heian International, Inc.
P.O. Box 1013
Union City, CA 94587

Originally published by Poplar Publishing Co., Tokyo

Translated by D.T. Ooka

ISBN: 0-89346-258-6

Printed in Japan

The Adventures of the One Inch Boy

Issun Boshi

retold by Essei Okawa

illustrated by Teruyo Endo

Heian

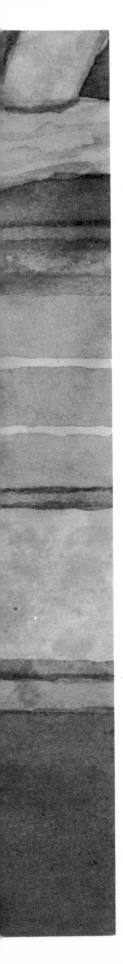

Long, long ago in a little village in Japan there was an old couple. They were very lonely because they had no children. Day and night, they would light candles before the family shrine and clap their hands to call the gods. They chanted, "Oh, gods above, please hear our prayers! We want a little baby so badly. Please give us a baby—we will love him and care for him even if he's only as big as a finger!" Even though the old couple sometimes did not have enough food to eat, they never forgot to pray.

Suddenly one day a tiny baby boy was born. He was only as big as a finger, but he cried with a loud, healthy voice. The old man and old woman were truly amazed! The old woman said to her husband, "Isn't this wonderful? Let's hurry and give him a name!" Joyfully, the old man replied, "We will call him Issun Boshi—the One Inch Boy, because he is no bigger than my finger."

The old woman sewed some tiny kimonos and the old man made a
cradle no larger than the palm of his hand. They raised Issun Boshi
with much love and care, and never forgot to thank the gods for their
little boy.

One, two, then three years went by, and Issun Boshi was still the same size he had been on the day he was born. Even after another seven years had passed, Issun Boshi had grown no larger. He never got sick and was healthy in every way except for his size. His elderly parents worried and prayed, but there was nothing they could do but love and care for him.

Now Issun Boshi was ten years old. He loved to go outdoors and play, but the other children made fun of him. They called him "shrimp" and "shortie" and would not play with him. Every day Issun Boshi went home very sad and lonely.

One day Issun Boshi went to his parents, knelt down, and bowed respectfully. "Mother, Father," he said, "I would like to travel and explore the world. Will you please let me go?" His parents were very surprised. "How can a little fellow like you go on a journey by yourself? Even the other children who make fun of you would not consider travelling all alone!" Issun Boshi replied, "That's exactly why I want to travel and see the world. I want to prove that I can do it myself! Please, please let me go!" Issun Boshi begged and pleaded until his parents finally gave in. "All right, all right," they said, "but be very careful! Come back to see us as soon as you can!"

Issun Boshi's mother gave him a sewing needle to use as a sword. He sheathed it in a piece of barley straw and tied it at his waist. Next she gave him a soup bowl and a chopstick. Issun Boshi wore the bowl as a hat and used the chopstick as a walking stick. Bidding his parents goodbye, he started off on his journey.

It was a beautiful, warm spring day. Issun Boshi walked through a wheat field, but soon lost his way. He met a kind brown dog who said, "If you go this way, you will only walk deeper into the wheat field. Walk towards the dandelions, and you'll soon come to the tall grasses at the edge of the field."

Issun Boshi thanked the kind dog, and walked through the dandelions and into the tall grasses. Once more, he lost his way.

Issun Boshi kept walking, determined to find a way out of the field. He came upon an ant, and politely asked her if she knew the way out. The kind ant led Issun Boshi to the edge of the field, where a tiny stream flowed.

Issun Boshi thanked the kind ant for her help. Then he used his soup bowl as a boat and his chopstick for an oar and floated merrily down the stream. Two bees and four butterflies flew by overhead. They called, "Little boy, be careful! At the third bend of the stream you will come to a great river which flows from the capital!" Sure enough, after the third bend the stream flowed into a larger river.

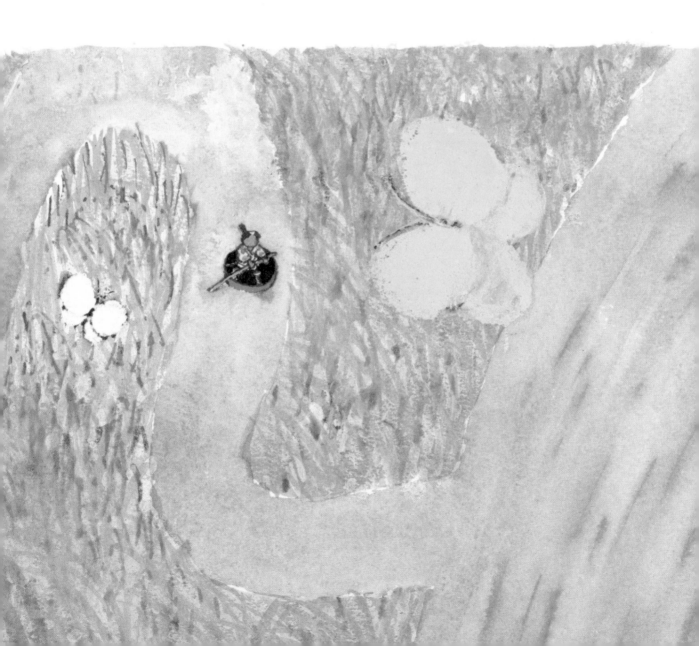

Issun Boshi thought it would be interesting to visit the capital city, so he began to row upstream. Gathering all his strength, he rowed as hard as he could with the chopstick oar and slowly made his way against the current.

After a long, tiring journey, the soup bowl boat finally landed at the base of the busy bridge. The bridge was crowded with ox-carts and many elegantly dressed people. Issun Boshi saw a tall five-storied pagoda surrounded by many houses with tiled roofs. He could only stare in wonder at all the marvelous sights. As Issun Boshi climbed up the riverbank, he thought, "I'd better find the most important person in the city!"

As he walked through the busy city, Issun Boshi came to a huge mansion. It looked like an important person's house, so he entered the front gate. "Excuse me, excuse me, is the master here?" he called in a loud voice. A servant appeared, but he saw no one at the gate. Scratching his head, he left, thinking he had been hearing things. But once again came the loud voice, "Excuse me, excuse me, is the master here?" Once more the servant returned, determined to solve this mystery. As he looked all around, he saw a tiny child standing next to a pair of wooden clogs. Wearing a soup bowl for a hat, the little boy was no larger than his finger!

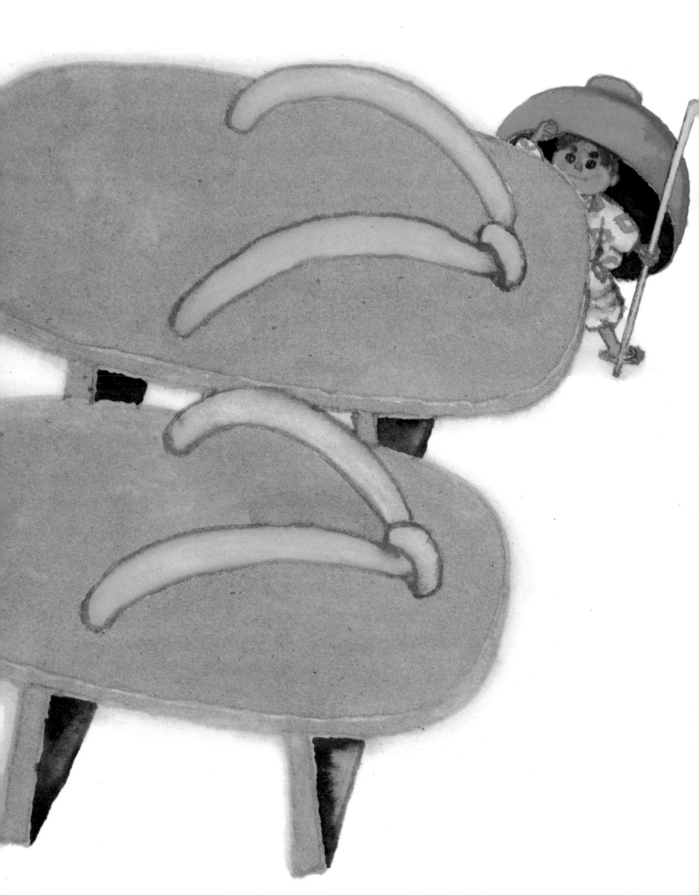

The entire mansion was soon thrown into an uproar, and Issun Boshi was brought before the daughter of the lord. She was the most beautiful princess he had ever seen! She held out her hand and said, "Here, hop up on my palm and tell me your name." Issun Boshi jumped up and replied, "I am Issun Boshi. I have come to this city to study and learn about the world."

The princess smiled and said, "Well now, little fellow—there is much to study here in the capital. You must learn to read and write before you can learn about the world." Issun Boshi realized that what she said was true, and made up his mind to study hard.

From that day on, Issun Boshi lived at the mansion and studied. He learned how to read, write, dance and play the hand drum. He practiced his swordmanship in the halls and gardens of the mansion.

The princess became very fond of Issun Boshi. She always kept him by her side, and whenever she went out, he accompanied her. Many happy years passed in this way.

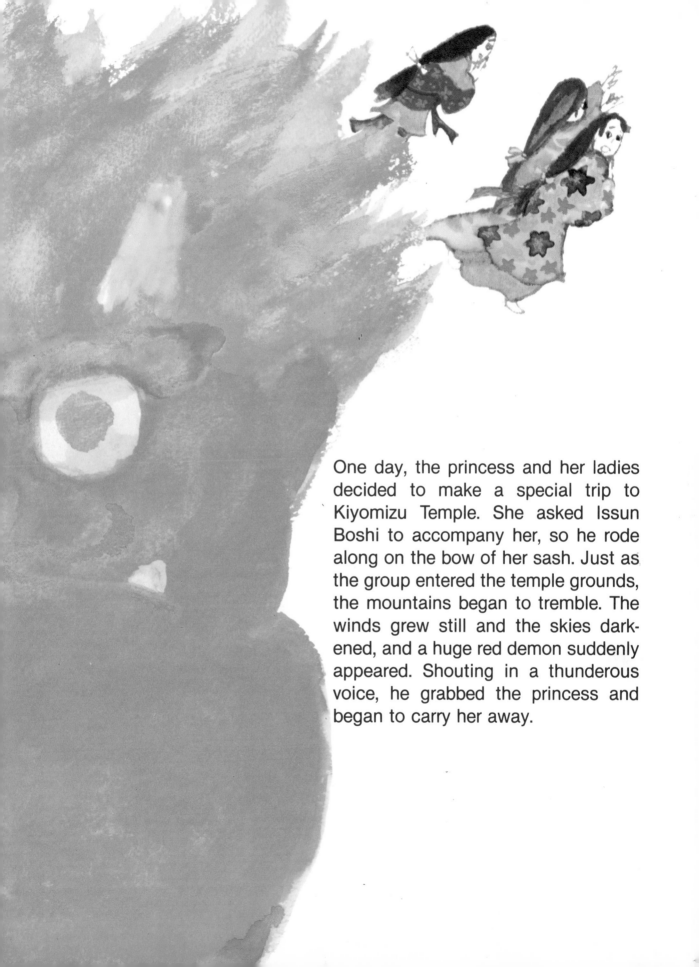

One day, the princess and her ladies decided to make a special trip to Kiyomizu Temple. She asked Issun Boshi to accompany her, so he rode along on the bow of her sash. Just as the group entered the temple grounds, the mountains began to tremble. The winds grew still and the skies darkened, and a huge red demon suddenly appeared. Shouting in a thunderous voice, he grabbed the princess and began to carry her away.

Issun Boshi jumped down from the princess' sash. He cried in his loudest voice, "You, big demon! You can't get away with this. Get ready to fight!" The big red demon looked down at Issun Boshi and burst into laughter. "What? A shrimp like you wouldn't even make one mouthful for the likes of me!" The demon picked up Issun Boshi, opened his mouth wide and swallowed him in one gulp. The poor princess was so terrified she could not make a sound.

Issun Boshi refused to give up. He drew his needle-sword and began to stab at the red demon's stomach. Stunned, the demon fell to the ground, clutching his painful stomach. He cried, "Stop, stop, little shrimp! You're hurting me!" But Issun Boshi continued to slash away—and soon he popped out of the demon's nose! Then he began to poke at the demon's eyes. The demon became totally helpless, wailing, "Ouch, ow, ow! My stomach is torn to shreds and now I can't see!" He ran off as fast as his legs could carry him, deep, deep into the mountains.

As the demon fled, he dropped a strange, glowing mallet on the ground. The princess picked it up and said with a smile, "Look, Issun Boshi! This is a demon's most precious possession—his magic mallet! If you make a wish when you wave this mallet, your wish will come true. What do you want, Issun Boshi? You may ask for money, rice, or anything else you desire!" Issun Boshi promptly replied, "I don't want money, nor do I want rice. All I want is to grow taller!"

The princess waved the mallet in the air as she chanted, "Grow taller, Issun Boshi, grow taller!" As the princess waved the mallet, Issun Boshi grew taller and taller. In an instant, Issun Boshi had become a handsome young man!

The princess' father, the important lord of the mansion, was greatly pleased that Issun Boshi saved his precious daughter from the red demon. He was so grateful that he decided to let Issun Boshi marry the princess. This made them both very happy.

Issun Boshi went to visit his elderly parents, and told them all of his adventures. They were overjoyed to see their son grown into such a fine young man. Issun Boshi was very happy to learn that his parents were still in good health, and brought them back to the city with him. After his return, Issun Boshi and the princess were married. Issun Boshi, the princess, and his parents lived together in the great mansion happily ever after.

AFTERWORD
by Essei Okawa

Issun Boshi is a very old tale that can be classified both as a fairy tale and a folk tale. It teaches the virtues of good deeds and exemplary behavior. Issun Boshi illustrates the strong bonds that bind parent and child as his parents raise him tenderly—a bond that the common people sought to strengthen between parents, children and grandchildren. It also illustrates the ideal of filial piety as Issun Boshi brings his elderly parents to live with him "happily ever after."

Although tiny, Issun Boshi exemplifies many characteristics of the folk hero. He never gives up despite his size and goes out into the world to prove himself; he does not retreat from a dangerous situation but uses his knowledge and strength to prevail; finally, he works not for personal glory but for the good of his parents and society. Thus *Issun Boshi* becomes a tale that emphasizes the many qualities prized by the Japanese people.